REFRIGERATED

MUSIC FOR A

GLEAMING

WOMAN

REFRIGERATED MUSIC FOR A GLEAMING WOMAN

STORIES

AIMEE PARKISON

FOREWORD BY
STEPHEN GRAHAM JONES

TUSCALOOSA

FC2 is an imprint of The University of Alabama Press

Inquiries about reproducing material from this work should be addressed to the University of Alabama Press

Book Design: Publications Unit, Department of English, Illinois State University; Director: Steve Halle; Production Assistant: Jade Urban

Cover Design: Lou Robinson

Typeface: Garamond

Library of Congress Cataloging-in-Publication Data

Names: Parkison, Aimee, 1976- author.
Title: Refrigerated music for a gleaming woman : stories / Aimee Parkison.
Description: Tuscaloosa, Alabama : FC2, [2017]
Identifiers: LCCN 2016039981| ISBN 9781573660600 (softcover) | ISBN 9781573668712 (ebook)
Classification: LCC PS3616.A7545 A6 2017 | DDC 813/.6--dc23
LC record available at https://lccn.loc.gov/2016039981

CONTENTS

FOREWORD

The best fiction ruins other fiction for you, for a while.

This fiction you're now holding—apologies in advance, but, for a couple weeks here, everything you read is going to come off as maybe a bit flat? Maybe a bit hollow? Maybe not as sincere as you were wanting it to be?

It definitely won't be as shot through with hilarity as *Refrigerated Music for a Gleaming Woman*. If the book's even comedic at all, I mean. I'm not at all sure it is. Could be that it's just honest. In which case, it's actually terrifying, and I'm thankful it comes in such small bites. All the same, reading this, you do grin. But a grin doesn't always mean something funny happened, does it? You grin grinding up the backside of a rollercoaster. You grin right before the plunge. You grin so you won't scream, and then you probably scream anyway.

The best fiction does that to you too. It kills you, then it pulls you back into the world, leaves you propped up in a corner, your smile not just pasted on, but sewn into place with an indelicate hand.

Or maybe it's just the invention here that works so well. I want to call it Borgesian, and want to conjure Donald Barthelme to bolster that, and maybe some Jack Pendarvis as well, but the delivery here, the sieve through which this imagination is strained.... I can't say I recognize it. I can't put a label on it. Even better? Each new and wondrous and awful thing that happens around every next corner of this book, never once is it what I'm expecting. Never once is it even in the *array* of things I would file under 'possible.' Yet each surprise occurrence, it's so completely organic to the—the voice? the world?—that I never feel cheated. You don't cry foul, reading this book. Yes, it pulls the carpet out from under your reading chair time and again, but from that first line, if you even halfway suspected you were on anything like solid ground, then that's on you.

However.

I'm making it sound all fun and games, all 'amusement park of literature.' That's just the wrapping I'm tearing through for you, though. Underneath, there's a real emotional core, a dynamo surging way down deep, a kind of font from which all of this springs, a—I'll go ahead and say it—a gravity drive using alien technology to warp us here, then there, then back again. The thing about gravity drives, though, is that the cost of this acceleration you're riding, it crumbles reality away, shimmers it into its next self. Go ahead, fight and claw your way down to that chamber. What you'll find is you can't look at this emotional core directly. It sidles ahead of your gaze, doesn't it? It makes you start to wonder what it's moving on: tentacles? roller skates? blood?

The best books leave you asking a lot of questions. The best books strand you in the doorway, just holding on, not wanting to leave where you know but being sucked through to this new place all the same. Once you peeled the cover back that first time, being sucked in was already a foregone thing.

Fight, of course—never submit, never surrender—but understand that this book doesn't only use force. It's seducing you the whole time. And not just with the fineness of its writing. Any fiction that tries to crutch along on brains and literary pyrotechnics like that, it should go by some other, lesser name. *Refrigerated Music* would never stoop so low. Yes, it is finely written, but fine writing is something we can just assume the presence of. Something we can expect, yes? Anyway, *Refrigerated Music* doesn't want to draw that kind of attention to itself. It would rather you forget you're reading. Really? I suspect that one of its seduction tactics is to let you, the reader, start feeling complicit here. That this is your secret journal, the one mined from your previous selves and collated, disguised, left in your path like a dead bird. One with a smaller, live bird tucked inside.

Stomp on that secret bird quick. If you don't, it's going to flutter up, crawl into your mouth, inhabit your brain, leave you a fetal little bean inside yourself, drifting through lives, sometimes peeking out through other eyes, sometimes just hiding.

The best books, they take you over just exactly like that, but then they wrap you in themselves at the same time, they fold you into a darkness sparkling with life. They lock you in the refrigerator but they also pipe in some music that never repeats, and when the door starts to open, you cling tight to it, so you can have just a few minutes more.

This book, it'll be over far too fast for you, yes. But even were it five times as thick as it is now, it would still be too short.

Remember, though, the best books, they're loops. They never stop.

This one still hasn't, for me.

We're locked together, we're circling some big drain, we're skating along the event horizon of an improbable event, we're running hand in hand along the rim of a killer volcano. Whether we finally spiral in together or not doesn't matter. What does matter is that we're smiling.

You will be too.

—Stephen Graham Jones

REFRIGERATED MUSIC FOR A GLEAMING WOMAN

CODE VIOLATIONS

When we were young and lived in the city, our first apartment was the size of a closet and once had been an actual closet, only recently converted into its own separate unit. The toilet had been installed inside the shower, located inside the makeshift kitchen, which was also the bedroom and the living room, as well as the dining room. The shower functioned as the kitchen sink, as well as the bathroom sink, located beside the stove. The television faced the shower. With this arrangement, you or I could take a shower and sit on the toilet while cooking dinner and watching pirated cable, all at the same time. Too convenient to be hygienic, the bed was also the kitchen table, which functioned as the sofa.

This design brought us closer during the early years of marriage, when there was no such thing as boundaries. By saving space and money, we came to know each other more intimately than most couples ever could imagine. That apartment, in spite of code violations, was the most romantic place we ever lived but also the cheapest and the most illegal.

You loved me better because of the toilet in the shower.

You were more committed to our relationship because of the shower near the stove. The heat of our food cooking warmed us even when we were naked, dripping wet from washing our hair with dish soap.

In the illegal design, I found innovations that excited me, improving the quality of our sex lives. I could cook soup while you were sitting beside me, relieving yourself on the toilet as I watched you shower.

Then, there was the other door that opened onto no room. Nothing but a tiny window that faced a dance studio with a theater below. We could open that door and stick our heads out to watch ballet together, free of charge. If we listened hard enough, we could hear a woman howling. Her screams were music through traffic.

TO SEE
THE HUMMINGBIRDS
AS THEY FLY
THROUGH THE TREES

Perpetual outsiders like me love to eavesdrop. That's how I heard her. Tonight, the howling lady to the tree said, *thank you for shelter.* Inside our house, she looks at the ceiling when hunting the gray-feet shadows climbing up the walls. You, my love, grind a tick against her neck and call it acquaintance murder. You never learned how to see her, to really see her, as you see me, while gazing into that antique mirror where I was a disappointment of skin like the rest of my family.

◊ ◊ ◊

Blindsided by the sea, the howling woman was one of many tattered war brides who became memories tossed away with letters. The letters were like gull feathers that floated along the water to navy men who became one with the sea.

◊ ◊ ◊

Hearts will be broken like windows, she said, by vandals, by time, by hail, by earthquakes, by thieves, by fire, by young boys.

◇ ◇ ◇

This sorrow is part of civilian life where dead women feud like prisoners of war, not knowing they are ghosts.

◇ ◇ ◇

Why do wars bring lovers together? Someone has to tell the living that torture is sometimes sexual the way a hearse can be mistaken for a limo.

◇ ◇ ◇

Love can be mistaken for lust.

◇ ◇ ◇

Hunger takes over. Who knows the truth about the hummingbirds?

◇ ◇ ◇

Hummingbirds enter the narrow bell-shaped petals of trumpet flowers as they feed, and yet the rest of us have to keep reminding the lovers that people are beheaded in burn cages as video cameras capture the moment for all to see. Someone who matters enough to kill and enough for us to watch them die again and again should matter enough to bury, yet it's so hard to find the graves just as it's so hard sometimes to see the hummingbirds as they fly through the trees. The green hummingbirds' feathers are the color of the leaves. As the lovers kiss, I want to fall in love with you. Something stops me in the leaves where we walk. Images of the beheadings enter my head the way the hummingbirds enter the flowers of the trumpet vines.

◊ ◊ ◊

As the howling lady becomes silent, we eat fast food
and watch videos of people dying by fire; again and again,
we watch on YouTube. You stuff hamburgers into your big
beautiful American mouth. I try to shut it out of my mind,
to think of the hummingbirds, the lovers kissing as the men
scream and the howling woman begins to sing.

FAST FOODIE

This hamburger train is like a bus but bigger. There's not going to be a bunch of intellectual people standing around talking nice. What did you think it was going to be? Eat your French fries in your Bliss Meal. Enjoy the toy. You paid for the free toy, that's why it's free. Please, god, whatever you do, don't open the hamburger. Don't look under the bun. Not at Mack-Dawn-A-Dolls. There's a reason we call the special sauce "special." Without it, you might see the meat, and this is the worst thing—to actually look at the meat and to start to wonder what it really is.

◊ ◊ ◊

Is this, really? The meat eaters say, Is this what meat's supposed to look like? What are these little flecks of aqua color in the beef? What is this beef made of, if it's not made of meat? Only a fool would want to know. If it tastes good and is cheap, eat it. Don't ask questions about fillers.

◊ ◊ ◊

My mother was strict when it came to meat etiquette. Meat was sacred, especially hamburger. When my sisters and I were children, if we didn't want to eat all the hamburger, if we said we were too full and just wanted the toy, she said, "Just take off the bun and eat the meat. Just eat the meat."

◊ ◊ ◊

I can still hear her say, eat the meat. Eat the meat.

◊ ◊ ◊

"Eat the meat."

◊ ◊ ◊

"Just eat the meat."

◊ ◊ ◊

That's what she would say.

◊ ◊ ◊

And she would only be satisfied if her children would eat the meat. Not eating the meat was the greatest sin in my family of meat eaters.

◊ ◊ ◊

Meat, they said, makes you strong.

◊ ◊ ◊

But aren't we all made of meat?

◊ ◊ ◊

Aren't we all what we eat?

◊ ◊ ◊

My family loves cheap meat, especially Mack-Dawn-A-Dolls. Now, they threaten to shun me. Because I don't anymore. I refuse to ride the hamburger train.

◊ ◊ ◊

Some fast foodies who begin to fear hamburger joints start to eat elsewhere, especially buffets. "Beware of Asian buffets!" My mother says, "You don't really KNOW what you are eating sometimes."

◊ ◊ ◊

My sister says, "Me and my kids went today. It was really delicious. The prices were amazing. We will be back."

◊ ◊ ◊

My girlfriend says, "I went last Wednesday. The food was very good."

◊ ◊ ◊

My father says, "I've seen the restaurant in front of Home Depot. I'll have to give them a try."

◊ ◊ ◊

My friend says, "My family and I have been a couple times. Great food, good price. But on the weekends, they don't have enough servers and busboys. The restaurant lost customers because of lack of service."

◊ ◊ ◊

My pastor says, "My wife ate there with some friends a few weeks ago and enjoyed her meal. We were there twice this month and enjoyed it very much. Everything was kept stocked, and hot things were hot while cold things were cold. Our table was bused and drinks refilled. It was delicious. Great. Enjoyed it very much, especially the hibachi grill and the seafood."

◊ ◊ ◊

My proctologist says, "Yeah, I've been to that place twice. I took an out-of-town guest, and they enjoyed the varieties of food. Price is good for what you get."

◊ ◊ ◊

My mechanic says, "Eaten there a few times. The price is right! I prefer China Buffet, though, for the variety and the custom Pho."

◊ ◊ ◊

My workout buddy says, "It's convenient. I work next door at Big Lots. My husband and I went today and were quite impressed! The selection and quality of the food was great, service was impeccable, and you really cannot beat the price! We'll definitely go back!"

◊ ◊ ◊

My realtor says, "I went there with my wife. We loved it, and I am happy with the atmosphere that they have going on. Even though I don't know what we're eating sometimes, and this makes me afraid because we love the food and the price."

◊ ◊ ◊

I want to warn them that if they don't know what they're eating, they shouldn't enjoy it so much. I want to tell them they focus too much on the cheap price and not enough on what they are putting inside their bodies. Then, I think better of it, because I don't know their financial situations. Besides, nothing is cheaper than Mack-Dawn-A-Dolls.

But what about the unfortunate who can't afford to eat the cheap meat at Mack-Dawn-A-Dolls?

◊ ◊ ◊

Cash-strapped fast foodies who can't afford to eat at hamburger joints should keep their eyes peeled in search of business opportunities, such as the ones I've been receiving in my inbox: *Do you pay a cell phone bill? Do you pay for Internet? Do you watch TV? Do you have electricity at your home? Natural gas? Do you use credit cards? If you answer YES to any of these questions, you are already in my business, you are just on the paying side. I get the privilege of teaching people how to get paid on these bills! Every month for the rest of your life! Residual income from now on.... It's just that simple. Contact me and I can show you how.*

◊ ◊ ◊

Because of my city's Anti-Feeding Ordinance, I no longer raid the dumpsters behind the Mack-Dawn-A-Dolls. I can no longer offer discarded hamburgers and unwanted meat to homeless people who wait outside my door. It was a good scheme while it lasted. I dove into Mack-Dawn-A-Dolls' dumpsters, stealing food. Now I'm facing jail time. In fact, the judge has just informed my lawyer that helping my city's homeless could land me in jail with a $2000 fine.

◊ ◊ ◊

Tell the mayor and the city council that feeding the homeless isn't a crime. Change the law and allow good Samaritans to feed the hungry with cheap meat.

◊ ◊ ◊

I was once homeless. I once relied on food from the dumpster. Because no one would feed me cheap meat for free, after my parents kicked me out of the house, I got a job at Mack-Dawn-A-Dolls while going to college.

◇ ◇ ◇

One day working as the drive-thru cashier changed my life forever. That day, I had the unfortunate task of informing one of our most loyal customers, a known serial killer and rapist who had been eyeing me for months, that we were out of baked pies. Baked pies were his favorite food. He went through the drive-thru every day, and ordered a dozen baked pies, cherry and apple. There were rumors in town. Baked pies were all he lived on. That's why he became a rapist, a murderer, a torturer, and the worst type of serial killer. Even though everyone suspected him whenever another woman went missing, there was no evidence to tie him to any crime. He spoke to no one, except for the workers at Mack-Dawn-A-Dolls. Those who worked the drive-thru window and provided him with his bag of baked pies on a daily basis were the ones he depended upon.

◇ ◇ ◇

I had to run into the walk-in freezer to get more pies. The delivery guys had just finished putting our truck up. Huge stacks of boxes, poorly stacked fries, partially thawed, fell on top of me. I was trapped in the freezer. The sweat on my arms crystalized, gleaming like little pulverized diamonds. I started to hear music unlike any music I have ever heard before or since. I'm certain I could hear it at that moment because I was covered in sweat while trapped in a gigantic freezer with cheap meat. Even though I have no words for the sound in my mind, privately, I have always referred to it as "refrigerated music for a gleaming woman."

◊ ◊ ◊

This refrigerated music was the one miracle I ever experienced. This is how I've come to believe that miracles come from calamity. My devastation was the reason I heard the refrigerated music for a gleaming woman in that twenty minutes before anyone realized I was missing. In that twenty minutes, I heard the music, which I would never hear again. When the rest of the employees got to me, my sweat had frozen into my arm hair, and I was in shock, singing.

◊ ◊ ◊

My aunt, the newly promoted assistant manager of Mack-Dawn-A-Dolls, was trying to get medical help when the storeowner found me collapsed on the tile. He said, "Just stick her back in the drive-thru. She'll warm up there."

◊ ◊ ◊

My aunt looked stricken but had no choice. This was many years before the incident at the funeral home. Sadly, in spite of her kindness and her numerous good deeds, corpse desecration came to define her in the community. Mack-Dawn-A-Dolls wouldn't even offer her another job when she got out of jail, even after she had served her time and had been released early for good behavior. But I get ahead of myself. I meant to talk about the serial killer/rapist and his baked pies.

◊ ◊ ◊

12

"Baked pies," I kept saying that day as I warmed up in the drive-thru window. After being rescued from the freezer, I couldn't hear the refrigerated music anymore. But the serial killer/serial rapist was still waiting for his baked pies. So I started to run and slipped on a wet floor. I reached out to catch myself, and my left arm caught on a hot grill. My arm was burned. Badly. The managers had no first aid kit, no gauze, so they started yelling to the customers and even out the drive-thru window, "Is anyone a nurse or a doctor? Anyone have any medical training? Maybe a first-aid kit?" (The managers had been told, under no circumstances, to ever call 911.) The serial killer/serial rapist was the only one who had medical knowledge. He left his car in the drive-thru and stood over me, ordering around every employee in kitchen. "Bring me mustard," he said. "To treat the burn, give me mustard."

◊ ◊ ◊

(Yes, mustard.)

◊ ◊ ◊

He rubbed mustard over my burned arm, but that didn't stop my severe pain. So he said, "Bring me ketchup. Lots of ketchup. In packets, if you have them. And bring me mayonnaise, and barbecue sauce." He slathered my injuries with the stuff, and soon I started to smell like a hamburger—burnt meat covered in special sauce. I was howling in pain, but the smell of my burnt skin slathered with ketchup, barbeque sauce, and mayonnaise, now melting into me, was making me hungry. I groaned. He just looked at me, shook his head, and said, "Bring me pickles, diced onions, and cheese—sliced thinly." My aunt and the other workers brought him the pickles, the diced onions, and the cheese, which he started to apply to my burns.

◊ ◊ ◊

"You've saved her," my aunt said. "Oh my god, thank you so much, sir. You've saved her." I was trying to tell my aunt who he was and that he hadn't really saved me at all because the pain was different now, throbbing, swelling like a serious infection. But she just kept calling him my savior and gave him a sack of baked pies.

◊ ◊ ◊

Later that day, a friend of mine, also working at Mack-Dawn-A-Dolls, saw my fingers were turning blue on the burned arm, which was now huge with swelling and festering blisters, yet still covered in pickles, cheese, diced onions, mayonnaise, mustard, barbeque sauce, and ketchup. My friend told my aunt, the corpse desecrator, that we were going to the ER. "Make sure you both clock out before leaving," said my aunt, and my friend drove me to the ER with my aunt's blessing. At the hospital, I was treated, given morphine for the pain. I struggled to feed myself with stolen hamburgers that smelled like my burnt arm. I hadn't eaten meat for such a long time, but because the smell of my burnt flesh was making me hungry, I gave in and tucked into stolen hamburgers, which tasted so damn delicious they made my tongue ache.

◊ ◊ ◊

The next day, when my friend and I returned to work at Mack-Dawn-A-Dolls, we were advised by my aunt that we had both been fired for leaving our jobs. My aunt was in tears.

I asked for a copy of that day's logbook entries, and to my surprise, that page was missing. How could a page be missing in a preprinted book with page numbers at the top corners? The log had skipped an entire two-day spread. Other entries had been re-written with the accident completely left out. I collected statements from former co-workers who knew what had happened. Later, they privately asked that I not submit their statements. They were terrified of losing their jobs.

◊ ◊ ◊

I tried to pay the $20,000 bond when my aunt was jailed after entering the funeral home. Placing a raw burger on the face of her boyfriend's deceased ex-girlfriend, another Mack-Dawn-A-Dolls employee, my aunt applied mayonnaise, pickles, and ketchup to the face of her boyfriend's dead ex-girlfriend while the body was on display at a funeral home. She covered the corpse's face in sliced pickles, diced onions, sliced cheese, and numerous buns. Then she arranged fries artistically like greased white-gold flowers with spikey petals around the casket.

◊ ◊ ◊

My mother said, "The police interrupted her while she was flipping burgers over the coffin. She had a hibachi set up over the coffin. They arrested her. For that! She was charged with illegal dissection of a body." *Desecration, not dissection*, I wanted to say. Then, my mother informed me that, inexplicably, in addition to prepping the burgers and fixings, my aunt had cut the dead woman's hair and slashed the face from hairline to nose tip during the viewing at the funeral home. Preparing hamburgers for dinner again, my mother suggested that this part might have been unintentional, some sort of kitchen accident from cooking on a makeshift surface that wasn't "food safe."

◇ ◇ ◇

I was at my parents' house, watching it all on the evening news while everyone else in my family was eating. The police on television said, "The funeral director informed us that the deceased's body was in a viewing room when some friends and family came to pay their respects."

◇ ◇ ◇

My mother, who was trying to get me to eat a hamburger, said, "When the grieving family entered, they observed your aunt with her hands inside the casket. But they let her go on! They just stood there, waiting in line for their free hamburgers, not knowing what to do as she cooked those burgers on her hibachi over the open casket. Not believing their eyes, I guess. Maybe this is a different sort of crime—a food crime. I don't know. But they ate the hamburgers, so tell me, how could this be a crime? Tell me. The fact that they ate the burgers changes everything. It has to in any court of law, right? The police didn't even catch her until later, when she entered the dead woman's house."

◇ ◇ ◇

The dead woman, a thirty-year-old whose cause of death was not disclosed, once dated my aunt's current boyfriend, but police did not know of a motive for the desecration. The dead woman's makeup was smeared, and my aunt allegedly stole her shoes and replaced them with frozen baked pies.

She then went to the dead woman's home under the pretense that she was sent there to retrieve jewelry so that she could take it back and put it on the deceased for viewing. When officers arrived at the home, they found my aunt, who held a bread knife with pieces of bun and hair on it. I had seen that knife many times and even used it to prepare food for myself and others. Apparently, my aunt had used the knife, the bun, and the chopped hair to sculpt a sort of bread crown for the deceased's head. This, my mother said, was "normal," and we shouldn't judge my aunt as "everyone grieves in her own way."

◊ ◊ ◊

"Your aunt has been arrested," my friend said when I returned to the old neighborhood for a visit. I pretended like I didn't already know when my friend, the same friend who had been fired for driving me to the ER all those years ago, tried to explain it to me, using clinical and forensic terms like "the deceased."

◊ ◊ ◊

"Apparently, people complained to the funeral home manager that the woman's body had been vandalized. The deceased woman's mother told officials that she discovered your aunt near the corpse with her hands in the casket. As the dead woman's mother walked towards her, your aunt then removed her hands. It was then that the family discovered what had happened to the corpse. Weird, huh?" I didn't say anything about the hamburgers. I hoped and assumed that part hadn't made the news and wasn't yet public knowledge.

◊ ◊ ◊

Because my friend stopped telling the story, as if he couldn't force himself to continue, to say what he knew, I started saying annoying things like, "What? What did they see? What happened to the corpse?"

◊ ◊ ◊

"Officials found hair on the floor near the woman's casket. Her makeup had been smeared and a large cut had been made from her hairline to her nose. Probably because of the bread crown. And she was covered in fixings."

◊ ◊ ◊

"Fixings?"

◊ ◊ ◊

"Condiments. Law enforcement officers discovered your aunt at the deceased lady's home with a box cutter, makeup, Bliss Meal toys, as well as a folding knife with the deceased woman's hair on it. Your aunt is now facing a misdemeanor charge of illegal dissection of a human body. Can you believe that? Being held on a $20,000 bond."

◊ ◊ ◊

I act like I have no idea, even though I'm really out collecting money for my aunt's bail, when another friend, who's now living in "the farms," shows me pictures of a man lurking on his porch at night and eating Mack-Dawn-A-Dolls while looking into my friend's window at 9:30 p.m.

◊ ◊ ◊

"This rascal came to the house three times," my friend says. "He appears to be pleasuring himself in the pictures, while also eating a hamburger. Is it even possible? Do my eyes deceive me? I mean, I've heard of multitasking, but this is a whole new level. Is it possible to put the burger down, for like three seconds? Thank god he has two hands so he doesn't have to make any difficult decisions."

◇ ◇ ◇

My friend gives me the pictures from his security camera to take around to his neighbors. He wants me to go door-to-door with him. Of course, I agree.

◇ ◇ ◇

I recognize the man in the photographs as my aunt's boyfriend, but I don't tell anyone, not at first. I need some time to think.

◇ ◇ ◇

"Please, please everyone look out for each other," my friend Russell says while taking the photographs door-to-door.

◇ ◇ ◇

"These photos are rather blurry. Any chance you could get a detailed description of the suspect from your friend so we can spot him before he approaches another house?" a lady asks.

◇ ◇ ◇

When I call my aunt's boyfriend, he says, "Y'all never gonna catch me."

◇ ◇ ◇

"What is he talking about?" my friend asks, and I keep telling him we need to look out for each other. Meanwhile, my friend says he's hungry. The photographs are making him crave a hamburger and fries, and he wants to go to Mack-Dawn-A-Dolls for an early lunch because the guy in the photographs really seems to be enjoying his hamburger. And I think that's just the thing about fast food, it's an addiction. Once we've taken the first bite, we're all fast foodies for life. There's nothing that can stop us from wanting more, even though we know we're destroying ourselves. The guy in the photographs is even making me hungry, even though I don't eat meat anymore, or at least I haven't since the time my burned arm made me hungry. I'm starting to want to eat meat again because of that look of absolute pleasure on the pervert's face. I still remember the taste.

REFRIGERATED
MUSIC FOR A
GLEAMING
WOMAN

Unemployed at the cryptic waterfront, my midway melody girl finds the music box enclosing a picture of the gleaming woman. Music again, a substance infused with god. Like a worshiper covered in blood, I consume god when I breathe the breath of the bandit educated at Harvard, what my love implies to poverty.

◊ ◊ ◊

Kissing him in the night after kissing you turns into majestic bathing, enigmatic water undone, our desire hurting him, hurting me like light, his body jeweled, like yours. My gleaming woman knows the significance of giving a god a drink. My friend, the wine pourer, remembers baby things, sex across the room. Enough despair, you said during a spontaneous orgasm, pouring out a mysterious drink to the gods, who would then listen to us at the ceremonial fire. [A brief explanation of why a woman like me has the balls to believe in spontaneous female orgasms: Ancient Israel was a land of vineyards, like my home. King David's wine collection was so large he had a special guard to watch over it. In the storerooms of the ancient wine cellar, my muscles so alive, I was like a bullfrog landing on a bible.]

◊ ◊ ◊

We were like two women who went into the mountains, two women who went into a ritualized trance, leaving the city of excessive drunkenness. In most early cultures, the making of alcohol was confined to women who taught priests the dangers of wine.

◊ ◊ ◊

Dehumanizing Joseph with booze was hotel policy for the dock workers, wandering toward pretty women who became like men in Vancouver, searching for watery graves, along with my bandit, like a priest killing turtle doves, ripping off their heads and setting them on fire so the bloody death could lead to atonement.

◊ ◊ ◊

Though I had just one god, I had to find a way to talk to her, a way to get a busy god's attention. The knife path is an important part of the ritual because wine is a portal to the past that devolves into sheer orgy captured in graffiti on the temple walls.

◊ ◊ ◊

The hotel walls were papered with vintage comics the bandit's great-grandfather read as a small child surviving the nightmare of smallpox, little roses blooming across his body, scarred. Thrush, how it feels to lose what they love. Selling family heirlooms on consignment. The boy's rotting name struck dead under her dress, like the kisses of a different husband. On his back, in his eyes, stillness with rage. Roughly, my children.

◊ ◊ ◊

In the days of smallpox, mothers delirious with the epidemic odors of sick rooms would save the scabs of dying children and would mail those scabs to mothers with healthy children. These scab mailers read the bible to the bandit's great-grandfather when he was a mere child, hiding under the bed of his sick brother, hiding in shadow and shy as the deer that gathered at the edge of the woods. In morning's mist, the grieving mothers collected the scabs of their dying children like manna from heaven.

◊ ◊ ◊

I have heard their songs, the lullabies to their dying children, still singing, all these decades later.

◊ ◊ ◊

Releasing refrigerated music, the gleaming woman shows them how it feels to lose what they love in a country once filled with slaves, her picture a thing to terrify ministers masquerading as masters. She speaks the boy's rotting name to a different husband, his dark into her.

◊ ◊ ◊

Silkily, I traffic in refrigerated music for the gleaming woman.

◊ ◊ ◊

The bandit has olive skin. His lips roughen in the dark-room where he kisses me deeply while he raises himself on his elbow. In his eyes, a different husband in the dark tried to relax my muscles. It was my fault. Wineglasses shattered on the darkroom door. Her picture, the only evidence we had of the gleaming woman. Her skin like powdered sugar, her eyes the color of oolong as he fed me croutons of bread dipped in the buttermilk of despair. I ate it all. I chewed until my jaw hurt. Still her gleaming, her hair of henna.

◊ ◊ ◊

It has to happen this way. Her picture implies a cage door: a suspected man hiding as darkness fell, ready to kill me at a moment's notice. Everyone is expendable except for the gleaming woman.

◊ ◊ ◊

She opens the darkroom refrigerator. Inside, bottles and jars, cold, appear empty. She opens one jar to release refriger-ated music. Closing the refrigerator door, she saves the rest for later as the music might spoil over time for those not alive to hear it in the moment it was played. The bandit, like his ancestors, steals sounds for her, and she saves stolen sounds behind the refrigerator door.

◊ ◊ ◊

I open the refrigerator to sample the music. Inside an-tique jars—Beethoven playing piano, slaves singing for free-dom in plantation fields, mothers humming lullabies to small-pox babies, humming through the night, knowing this song is the last sound their children will ever hear.

THE NOMAD

When the music starts, look into the mirror and make
that clueless face, sweat on your lips glittering like salt on the
dancer's skin. The dancer is a young President Reagan lost
in a mutant Disneyland wearing your old nightgown like a
dishrag.

◊ ◊ ◊

The man in the next room uses a synthesizer to create his
songs behind the walls. The songs are what you remember,
long after you forget the dancer's eyes and Reagan's erection,
along with the rest of what's better left forgotten.

◊ ◊ ◊

How could you have explained to the dancer how you
really felt about him? Who you really are?

◊ ◊ ◊

There's no way of saying.

◊ ◊ ◊

You're a lesbian in love in the desert of youth, where cocaine sex created a moral panic in vast Texas towns, an usurpation relativistic like justifiable homicide on the breaking news.

◊ ◊ ◊

Your first female lover called herself "the nomad." Her cunt was a benevolent wound that whispered past the word boundary, a seducer's rhythm, subterranean in the cross currents of her come cry, the glottal pulse palatial, breathing phonation like a palpable intoxicating backwoods moral panic, the gallows of provincialism. With her cronies, she started her own Mickey Mouse Club, a cartoon caricature of muckraking crack babies, pink eyed with their unwed mothers. Children in their own right, they spread syphilis like prophecy.

◊ ◊ ◊

Love child to love child, their velvet lust was like yours— a relic, liminal, yet contagious like consumption.

RESPONSIBILITY

Eat the meat, my mother says. Eat it with a big glass of milk, ice cold from the refrigerator, and a slice of American cheese. I want to tell her about the hidden-camera investigation I'm coordinating, using a video camera I stole from her and my father. But I fear she wouldn't understand because she's too American, like her cheese. Cheese is her weakness, and she thinks milk is mine, but she has no idea what I'm really into, what I'm doing with her stolen camera.

Drink your milk, she says, and I want to tell her about my hidden-camera investigation into the dairy industry. Sadly, I have uncovered a pattern of extreme cruelty, neglect, and violence by cows who have mistreated farmers. Because of the viciousness of milk cows, people have been exploited and forced to endure lives of constant misery and deprivation.

My videos reveal cows prodding farmers, cows threatening farmers with milking equipment, and cows punishing farmers by throttling them during milking.

Cows violently beat and kick farmers in their faces and bodies, leaving men and women with hoof marks, open wounds, and infections. Thanks to the ferocity of milk cows, farmers have been stabbed and viciously hit with milking equipment. Terrified farmers have been victims of tails, which cows have manipulated for several minutes at a time in order to "punish" the farmers.

Cows, spiteful and disgruntled, are caught on my videos. These are the thoughts I think at the dinner table while Mother and I drink to our health, having another big glass of milk, cold from the refrigerator.

HOT LUNCH PETITION

A hungry kindergartner came to my friend, the cafeteria worker, Macy Dolan, crying because she couldn't pay for her school lunch. Macy did what any cafeteria worker with a heart would do. She drove to the kindergartner's house and used a frozen pepperoni pizza to beat up the kindergartner's mother, who claimed the child should eat for free.

Unfortunately, the elementary school where Macy was employed has a policy against giving students free food. According to protocol, the situation is handled in this manner: the first three times a student is unable to pay, the lunch is taken to the bathroom by a cafeteria worker and flushed down the toilet before the child's eyes. The fourth time, the school provides a hat shaped like a cheese sandwich and milk.

Macy had seen the ridicule these children endure when their peers witness them wearing that cheese on a bun. She also saw these children's energy wane because they weren't being nutritionally sustained by flushed lunches. But what really bothered her was the way soggy pizzas began backing up toilets in the school restrooms. The melted cheese on the toilet rims, along with the pepperoni and tomato sauce swirling, pushed her too far.

Near cafeteria trash cans overflowing with squandered food, poor children huffed fumes of hot lunches the rich kids threw away. Soon, even rich kids began huffing hot lunches from the trash as they learned the fumes could get them high.

Unfortunately, we live in a country where rich kids are "kids" and poor kids are not "kids" but "children." We live in a country where food is flushed away by adults or trashed in stinking heaps by rich kids while poor children go hungry. Just to get by, poor children have to invent new ways for rich kids to get high. But everyone, rich or poor, has one thing in common, and that is the need for toilets.

That is why Macy Dolan uses food as a weapon, wielding a frozen pizza at the faces of the parents of hungry children. Now that she has been fired, she is calling on the School District to reinstate her for saving toilets sacrificed to childhood hunger.

A person who cares this much about toilets belongs in our schools.

THE CANDLE

When I was a child, I set my family's house on fire. I was nine years old. My father never forgave me. I lit a candle in the window to see the beautiful flame against the dark sky as I drifted to sleep in my bed. One moment, everything was fine, the flame glowing red against the night. The next moment, the curtain was on fire. I watched it burn. Flames leapt the curtain and began to climb the wall. My bedroom filled with black smoke. Mother was screaming for my father to wake up. Wake up, wake up, wake up! I ran down the stairs to find him sleeping on the couch in front of the television.

Even now when I visit my parents in the other house, my father sometimes looks at me like he's remembering why he can't forgive me. I'm now thirty-nine years old, and I want to tell him the fire moved so fast, so much faster than I ever expected fire to move.

In the interest of repairing our relationship, I want to explain what he'll never understand about that night, but something stops me. Perhaps I'll never understand what it was like for him to work so hard to pay for that house and everything in it, to fall asleep on the couch, watching television after a long day of work, and to wake to screams and the house filling with black smoke. What was it like for him to call the fire department and wait for them to arrive, to get me and my mother safely out of the house, and then to stand outside the house with the neighbors, watching the house burn? He was watching the neighbors watching him watching it burn, and then he was watching my mother's eyes changing when they told her it was too late.

The house was already too far gone by the time he looked at me.

THE SELF
AND OTHERS

My lawyer speaks for me because I'm losing control of my own affairs. I dream of murdering people, even though I'm not a violent person. In the attic, a trunk—a chest or box—I sometimes open while looking out the window at the garden gate because I can't bear to glimpse what Mother has locked inside. Near the staircase is a ladder to another window, a view of my neighbor's house—a window looking into another window of another's world. The ladder I'm afraid to climb for fear of going too high and looking into a room I'm not supposed to see. In the house, I'm drowning in narrow spaces with photographs lost in purses. As a child, I was the victim of a kidnapping. My captor was someone I knew. I will never say his name because I know him, even now. He was once a dear friend of my family, growing ever dearer and more frightening over time.

SNOW IN THUNDER

A delicate person in relationships, like most beaten women, you misplace your anger. In the days when I first moved like snow in thunder, you took your anger out on people in books you love, the reader in *belles lettres* with no critical light. The people in your books are real to you, but are also playthings. You once referred to me, your baby sister, as your plaything; it's hard for me to know this delicate touch like dust in pages of cloth books, disintegrating as music fades along with sky. I just gaze at ginger kittens staring out the window, the misty watercolor I want to live in. Following music, laughter, and light, I am the thing you love more than knowing my shadow steals. Dance with me, even though twenty years ago I didn't know what dancing was. Breathe deeply. My nose scents fried shrimp and rice cooking. I still walk like snow in thunder. Inside the house, why is Mother always Mommy? Don't ask. Jimmy tells everyone it's okay

Mommy pretends, searching for moon gleams, concrete rain, water falling over tunnels; and now with me, Jimmy cries for Mother at her funeral as we wonder why we have to hide. Just before sleep, put away all thoughts, memories of old friends, faces of the children in new light, soft skin, the dream where you hope to gain the truth about me, where I went when I disappeared in our childhood, as our dead mother goes on a diatribe about the spirit of work, health, happiness, domestic and private goals. She creates order from disorder when she says, *I'm the dust. If your sister had lived, she would have been snow in thunder.* Fists pound on walls, and you say to our father, *stop.* It's too late. Even though I still walk like snow in thunder, I hear thuds of delicate books falling, dishes breaking, boxes overturned. Sometimes there are no bruises, only words. Broken words are a lullaby, or a love song. How I long to caress even your sweet bones. Something deep inside you grows dumb, a hidden visitor you don't want here in winter. My words won't leave. Where we once clung for warmth in the rooms, broken heaters hiss near the swamp of shared plumbing, common bathrooms. Little gray puddles float our lost trinkets, pictures. Old pipes speak, children whispering.

THE CASTING
DIRECTOR

While naked in the hospital, Catherine, your name caught in the vortex of the movie business. Because Jackie's rooms were empty, we began to sublet them to men writing screenplays and found your agent's wacky clients floating around the halls.

There was a scream. (Finally Marion got off the phone.)

There was this young guy kind of hunched in a stooped posture, unattractive. One day I see this guy walking up the hall from Jackie's. Later?

Even I saw the marks of sexual terror on her body.

"If you can't change that, I think you should take my name off," you said. But by then the tattoo was already beneath my skin like a terrible love affair.

In those days, there was nothing but terrible love affairs, as if you loved feeling unloved. As if you were in love with the idea of being underused, womanly unwanted, ladylike castaway, girlish garbage, as if you were—Sick of feeling well, Catherine? And wanted your lovers to destroy your body because someone killed our friend Jackie in September.

I thought to myself *do this part*. Loving you will be the nail in my acting career and then I can do other things.

Even now, you keep your door locked so I can't talk to you. Even now, I want to say Jackie was murdered but can't afford to say. Even now, I can hear you say—in sexual matters, there is a medical truth. Don't say—Praying, just let her see me.

Actors were not freaks to me. They were people. Marion would look into Jackie's eyes.

Marion was always looking for you in Jackie's eyes. When I met Marion, she would look at you and you knew she was seeing something that you didn't want to see about yourself. My central essence that Marion saw was that I had a good amount of ignorance, a good amount from very powerful people.

The audition process is so disturbing like a pelvic exam. Like a question mark of how good you would look at the swimming pool. Women would get you undressed so men could make sure you didn't have any scars on your body. It was like the witch trials. Unsightly scars, no matter how beautiful they said you were, scars could hurt. Scars were marks from the devil. Women's flesh had to remain unmarred if they wanted to survive. You knew that from the beginning. You should have known after all you taught us.

◊ ◊ ◊

The man assisting me down there kind of owned the town. He took me upstairs to the little room with a little window, a little window where I could see his town. You weren't a part of his town, not then, and would never be again. That's what he told me as he inspected me for scars that might keep me from becoming a starlet.

I wasn't going to lie to you.

A person like you, not Marion, loves to eavesdrop until the men learn how to see her as a woman they knew long ago. There was one in particular, the hottest actor to hit Hollywood, his aquamarine eyes battered by California and all the young actors who met his description in the book.

God knows they were beautiful, you said to the man, Catherine, the one whose looks opened doors and legs everywhere and ruined him by allowing him to go into places inside other men where other men weren't allowed to go.

People who dreamed of mothering his illegitimate children were locked into you and what women like you had written on the page. Later, they were like your lovers in that battered hearse moving away from the hospital where you once wanted to recover. Recover from the uneasy bargain, the marks on your body, the unsightly scars you tried to camouflage with tattoos like bruises in the shape of your lovers' hands. Soon, it was hard to tell the difference between the bruises and the tattoos of bruises, the scars and the scarification. You were no longer in the little window. I couldn't see you anymore. You were hurting me in places I couldn't see. Catherine, your name caught. People are saying there's no way of knowing.

FOLLOW ME HOME

After a forest fire near the photographer's house in Malibu, an important decision is made about the homeless child I found—whether to take the child home or to take its picture, repeatedly. Secretly, after viewing crisp negatives of the child hiding under a bridge in the rain, the photographer confesses his pride is injured because the child will not trust a stranger following with a camera. For some reason, after I view these images, drinking merlot, I contemplate suicide, listening to a recording of live cello music. My overdose occurs during a concert late at night, after a thunderstorm as the child slumps under my balcony, waiting out the rain, still humming music I almost remember. Before my stay in the hospital, the child found me unconscious, barely breathing in a parking lot where I don't remember falling and where my car wasn't parked. I recover from exhaustion in early spring, after the images are developed, but the child refuses to follow me home because he is afraid of the photographs of naked women on the walls. He says he doesn't want to live with me inside the photographer's house. After a gallery opening, the photographer says he feels like giving up because something embarrassing happens to me (I cry) every time he tries to sell his tasteful photographs of the homeless child to wealthy clients, collectors—mostly older women searching for surrogate mothers. These women were once actors, models, beauty queens, trophy wives. They say they cannot carry their unborn children in their bodies, so the biological children made from their frozen eggs are always homeless and must search for other homes, needing the bodies of poor women to house them and carry them safely to the wealthy mothers waiting. All these women are photographed in the nude by my lover. He knows how to make them appear young again, even though they look twice my age when I tell them why the homeless child won't follow me home.

CHILD OF PRAYER

Blue-black hair, murals over a river, bridge-side guitarists strum their women, pass like visions. Saints and whores dance over dark water. Under a fresco of red stars, lust makes dreams come true. *She's the devil,* her father whispers, passing like a train through night. *She's a sick person and all her life will be sick.* He senses the child growing inside her forty years before it's born, taking time to come back to life, hanging its head, still wet, completely alone. He feels the jade beads of her eyes light on him, the other family frozen in time, immobilized by her youth, her hands passing over the cheap blouse. She's talking through allusions—her mouth tastes like money, ashes and dust moths, red wine, pulp slick with blood. *She's intelligent, but not pretty,* he said. *I warned you.* She dreams of Kahlo's self-portraits, eyes trained to express loneliness, cadmium hemorrhage. A rod inserted into the vagina teaches girls to dance like women. Their bodies sparkle, gold powder. She feels the need to bond to every person, telling details of her suffering. *I warned you*, he said. She didn't want to improve what God made ugly, the father who adored her fearful mystery. His pity passed, a hawk through night. *Every now and then remember the affection your father has always had for you*, lovely as blown glass, a symbolic space she could never truly inhabit. The details of her blackouts taken as a bad dream in firelight, strange shadow moving between her legs, fingerlike, long lines, heat lacing her thighs. Even in younger years, her skeleton is a sign of strength smoldering inside her—child of paper, straw, and clay. Hands trained to fend for themselves claw like dogs, stroke like fiends. Love is always, the far distance, the square leading out of the painting to the unseen cradle. She's attracted to women, breasts soft as her hands passing under thin blouses, palms cupped, fingers trembling, wrists free. *Dance*, he said, and she danced until he was gentled by the child as it kicked inside her. Wavering, she walked the house a shambles, her blood trail gathering darkness as she choked on a thin crust of bread. Waking takes all night. Semen flows like wine, breath of ecstasy, gentle torture. Men pass like sorrow, her women drinking alcohol, washing their jeweled nipples, their teeth clacking on bottlenecks. Trains carry sisters between two houses, linked by a bridge. She's the wounded one living in a blue house with imaginary friends, weightless, dancing, feeling at home in her haven, her lovers light as air as she weaves their wings of straw. Hilarious nights weeping songs of dark-haired women, the river that ran through her life. If her love were visible, she could paint it—how terrible to know nothing lies beyond, a child who went through a world of colors. *I warned you*, he said, and she promised to become a better painter. Starving herself, her head light as water in clouds, feeling the difference between night and day, elegant fingers stretched canvas, revising drawings. Scrawled captions begged strangers to remember her: dawn sky, girl with a ribbon tied around her waist, woman in white on the blue-house patio, a trained dancer, her naked arms outstretched. Hungry as mouths she wanted to feed, her hands moved over the child who gave her visions, fainting spells, night water. Tonight fingers fly over her eyelids like fireflies above the river. Child of strangers' dreams, she was the mother of gateways, infamous men waltzing over her back. Rambling trains passed like sisters in the night. *She's the devil*, her father said. *Take her and feel the workings of the world.* The sun and moon hold sway over her eyes, the plastic tiara resting on her hair.

THEFT PREVENTION 101

In warm weather, owners of used condoms bring them out of storage or garages, out onto the streets and parking areas. Unfortunately, these are high-theft items due to the ease of mobility. A small team of thieves can easily pick up and place a used condom in the back of a truck, van, or trailer within minutes. Unsecured used condoms are the first items to be stolen. There are no security systems or devices that are 100 percent foolproof; however, various devices and techniques can be used to deter, slow, or eliminate a used-condom theft from occurring.

The best technique is a method that has been in operation for centuries and, unfortunately, as a modern society, we have not kept up with; it involves getting to know your neighbors. When a used-condom collector communicates and gets to know his neighbors, it helps make others aware of when a suspicious individual may be lurking around a used condom a neighbor may own. A neighbor can then communicate quickly with the owner or 911 when suspicious activity is occurring.

Other techniques when away from home involve being aware of one's surroundings: parking in lighted areas where cameras are focused, checking regularly on used condoms, and securing used condoms to large anchors such as poles.

There are various methods of securing used condoms with cables and chains. While all chains and cables have the potential of being defeated, some are stronger and more reliable than others. If using a chain, we recommend using thick linked chains with a high-quality lock. Most chains up to ten milimeters, no matter how hard or what material is used, can be cut with a standard hardware store three-foot bolt cutter. Twelve- to thirteen-milimeter chains are much more difficult to cut, and keep in mind that chain links need to be cut twice. Sixteen-milimeter and ninteen-milimeter chains are the most difficult to cut with any hand-operated bolt cutter. Core-hardened chains, often called triple heat-treated chains, are the strongest types of chains, much more difficult to cut. Having a high-quality lock is also very important.

To reiterate, the best method of used-condom theft prevention is being vigilant of where your used condom is housed, stored, or displayed, along with getting to know one's neighbors. Making neighbors aware of your used condom collection can help everyone be aware of suspicious individuals in your neighborhood. Remember to call 911 when you witness suspicious people or activity in your community.

ABORTION

All you ever wanted was to hold me in your arms as if I were your real baby, so that you could stare into my eyes. If you could, you would be my salvation, if only for a day, when you could pretend I was never inside you, waiting to be born. The thing called nothingness, the thing you so desire to name, that thing is nothing without a name. The name you give me in hopes of creating a meaning becomes meaning. Taking on meaning with every stolen hour, your discovery of me becomes a discovery of you. That thing you may never see is only theoretical, no future could ever prove. All I know how to say is lost in this thing you call time, which is different from the time I once thought I knew, time you now say is linear so that once I say it once is over forever when all I ever wanted was ever returning to the beginning, rebirth renewed, a cycle. Life returning. If I'm really yours, I should know. Mother, I love you. Mother, I am part of your particles.

Mother, don't leave me. Mother born. Every time you displease me, threaten the future. The only necessary technology for abortions is a time machine. And yet, all you ever wanted was to hold me in your arms as if I were your real baby, so that you could stare into these eyes and know if you are my mother, then time would be your salvation, if only for a day, when you could pretend I was never inside you, waiting to be born.

LOVER WITH GUN IN MOUTH, OR AUTOPSY AFTER MURDER

An arrow of light, exquisitely his fingers move inside me, over petals in the meadow of flowers you once knew as my body. Though closest to him, I'm the one who tells him the police learned how to kill us tonight. You told me not to. I did it anyway.

◊ ◊ ◊

Drinking from cocktail glasses of suspicion, women will teach you to master the fine art of the unpredictable embrace.

◊ ◊ ◊

The children's food was always running out in a way that seemed cruel to him, even if they were raised in that part of the city forensic anthropologists called Trigger Way, where the rich world used what people looked like physically to define their characters.

◊ ◊ ◊

In the name of progress, even liberals began asking themselves at private benefits: *Can we fix the nose? Can we fix the teeth? We can teach them how to act? Give them dancing lessons, elocution lessons, teach them how to ride thoroughbreds so the police won't have to kill them?*

◊ ◊ ◊

Will it work if we try?

◊ ◊ ◊

People are saying there's no way of knowing.

◊ ◊ ◊

Intelligence is a disease. That's why my lover has a gun in his mouth.

◊ ◊ ◊

Moments after he's dead, a toilet against his neck where he fell, I realize he is our king. His death teaches us many things, how not to get shot by the police by shooting ourselves in the head before the authorities can read our faces. How great it is to live with a gun in the mouth in the leaves abandoned along with the wisdom of our king, the interloper.

◊ ◊ ◊

With a gun in the mouth, it's impossible to care if anyone is pointing a gun at you. You are free.

◊ ◊ ◊

Just living would be enough, unless you were born on a grave.

◊ ◊ ◊

Conversation is troublesome yet necessary like an autopsy after murder.

THE FIRE ESCAPE

Like vultures, reporters swarmed, even though my child had been dead for years. Knitting at the causeway, I had withdrawn only to tend to memories, to heal. Tenderness was bread crumbs on the windowsill, where I fed sparrows and watched them feed while hiding my face behind curtains. Please do not come, I said as I saw fear glittering in the eyes of the curious stranger, another reporter who had dared to enter my screened porch without invitation. An eight-year-old girl survived. He showed me. I saw her in the photograph, restored. Kidnapped from her family at the age of three, my child was the body discovered in the remoteness of small ponds and lakes. It had started to ruin. Cadaver dogs were released into the woods. No explanation for what had happened. All these years, our house on that land, vacant. Then came autumn, the rusted fire escape marked by footprints, someone going in and out of the house in secret.

ON FLOODED ROADS

Do not believe the kidnapped girl was still alive in the photograph, six miles away from where she was found, wrists bound, downhill in dense brush. The search ended in chaos, volunteers confused by highway patrol, cadaver dogs, a helicopter crashing before a storm, reporters and investigators with no logical explanation for what had happened. I saw the tracks. A volunteer, I always felt we had failed her. I've carried the guilt for years into the hills of Tennessee, along with the other searchers. Following tracks into the hills, we discovered the photograph on a broken card table inside an abandoned mountain cabin.

In the photograph, she was smiling, wearing the same clothes she was last seen in the day she was reported missing by her trucker father, some months before, when she "disappeared" in a violet hoodie and dark denim jeans, her hair in a sideways ponytail. The photograph showed her standing inside the mountain cabin in front of the picture window, as if posing in her ponytail, smiling for someone who held the camera. Behind her, the window revealed a view of autumn trees, yellow leaves golden in fall sunlight.

Through the window, when we, the searchers, looked out, those trees were the same, brilliant branches burning with umber splendor.

Who had taken the photograph? We wondered, even though we saw it as a positive sign, at least in the beginning. In the photograph, she appeared alive, happy. She was not alone, and we considered this a good thing for her at the time, even though it was possibly a bad thing. Now the searchers had to deal with a threat, an unknown. Our community felt invaded. We were a small, close-knit group, mostly church-goers not keen on strangers or on sympathizing with girls who ran away to be with strangers.

As the detective pointed out, who could be with her in the woods in the cabin, except a stranger? She might have run away to be with a man, someone using the cabin as a hideout. If she wanted to be with him, though, why was she scream-ing? Her voice, distant, echoed through the trees as we tried to find her.

Staring at the photograph, we thought we would find her in a remote area of lakes and ponds, dense and heavily wood-ed near the hills, the valley just behind the cabin surrounded by old-growth forest. While following the tracks through the trees, in the evening, we saw her running from us. In the dis-tance, she was screaming, again, her ponytail flapping crazily, as if she were terrified, horrified that we were attempting to rescue her.

By the time the detective saw her running, he was using his long flashlight at night to cut through the darkness.
There was much talk of a coming storm, forecast to bring
high winds, flash floods, and the threat of a tornado.

Explaining he needed to protect the searchers and this
"difficult decision" was "part of the burden of being in
charge," the detective said it was enough for one night, too
dangerous to continue.

To his credit, even though I disagreed, I should mention
the reasons for what he decided. Three searchers had already
been lost, two wounded by falls, and the helicopter crashed
into the trees, yet she was still running so fast, away from us,
weaving through the brush. It was almost as if she were playing a game, wanting to bring the searchers closer to harm.

We had to use machetes to clear the vines. We fought
the brush and branches, which tore our clothes. We called
her name, repeatedly, but whenever we got close to her in the
trees, she darted out of view.

◊ ◊ ◊

Sometimes, when we couldn't see her, we heard her
howling, as if calling for help. The howls were what I heard
when we were packing up, talking of going home.

"Watch out," the detective said. "She might not be as in-
nocent as she seems, not if she's running from us."

She was a delinquent, after all, the detective assured us.
A delinquent, and therefore, at least somewhat responsible
for her own fate. Besides, he said, she was probably out there
with the man she loved.

◊ ◊ ◊

When it came to the detective's thoughts about the man, whom he reasoned might be a criminal, I began to have my doubts. I argued with the detective, saying that his suspicions about the man were more of a reason to keep searching than a reason to give up. What do teenage girls know about men? I asked. What do they know about love, especially that type of love? I wanted to ask more questions about girls and men, but something in the detective's eyes stopped me. I remembered he had three teenage daughters.

"Even if she did it on purpose," I said, "even if she's with a man she thought she loved, do you think she understands the risks?"

"No," he said. "Not yet, no matter what she might have done. But there's nothing more we can do. Not tonight."

His face hardened when we heard the next scream and the trees were lit by lightning. She might have been playing games, he said, wanting attention, her name in all the papers.

"Especially if she's playing games, we need to look out for ourselves," he said. "There will be reports to file. I'm responsible. The city will be upset about the helicopter. The operator might not make it. There might be criminal charges filed—against her."

"I see," I said, even though I didn't.

"Girls who want to be rescued don't run from the police," he reasoned aloud.

"Are you sure?" I asked, but it had already started to rain, hard, and I could tell the storm would be a bad one, perhaps impossible for us to search through the flood. "Can't we just keep searching a few more hours?"

"Have a good night and get home safely, Miss," the detective said, his hair drenched in rain.

That night, more than anything, I realized how dangerous it was for girls to fall in love with men, especially the wrong sort of men. The wrong sort of man meant people would judge a girl's worth in a different way. Even the rumor of her loving a certain type of man was enough to condemn her.

◇ ◇ ◇

Reluctantly, I left the woods that night, along with the other searchers. None of us wanted to leave. We all thought she was still alive because we could hear her. We had no way of knowing what was happening, or why.

Days later, her remains were discovered. No one could believe the condition of her body, found by campers after the storm, washed into a drainage ditch near the woods where we had seen her. The corpse was in an advanced state of decay. "At least three months, any coroner could tell," the detective said.

I asked to see the photographs. Everyone who had been part of the search asked and was sorry to see, because who could forget that dead look in the face with missing eyes?

Even so, we had seen her alive in the first photograph, the one we found in the cabin. Saying it was a hoax, the detective filed that mountain cabin photograph as evidence. It would only hurt his case, especially as we had seen her rushing on the land, darting through the trees, terrified, near the place where her body had already ruined in the remoteness, cradled by trees, overhanging branches.

Following the thing mistaken for her, those tracks, her older sister was the first searcher who went missing. We couldn't find the sister searcher, and didn't, not until more than a year later, a year after the first body had been discovered.

A man of haggard beauty tried to burn down the mountain cabin just days before the sister's body was found. All these years later, I still remember how the night birthed panicked cries.

Don't say *amalgam*.

In the cupboard of the historical cabin, remains decayed, a human menace even in their deathtrap. A biohazard of luggage, stinking like a degradable puzzle, the suitcase waited to be opened, contents examined. This body was evidence, now a weapon to be used against her suspected killer.

At the police station, under psychological evaluation, accused of many more crimes, the haggard beauty would only say his name was Charles. Charles! That name appeared in all the papers, along with the photograph of his ruggedly handsome face, blue-eyed and movie-star gorgeous like James Dean in all the mugshots. No one could find out who he really was, or is. He would say only that there were others— women and girls. He would not say who they were, where he had taken them, or if any were still alive. Even if most of us in the community knew he was taunting us, I was one of the searchers who took the bait and began my own investigation into what might have happened.

◇ ◇ ◇

That was when I began to see you, to hear your voice in the woods, the way I heard the first girl's voice in these same trees. The instant I heard you, I knew what had happened. It was the same thing that had happened to her, and her sister.

◊ ◊ ◊

Don't be afraid of me. I want to help you. Don't be ashamed of what he has done to you and to the others. It's not your fault, and I won't judge you, even if you went with him willingly, at first.

These things could happen to any woman, any girl.

These things happen all the time.

However, searchers don't usually hear cries in the night, find photographs, or see the dead running.

Sometimes I wonder about the first girl, if she was the one who started it all, if it was her or her sister, but her sister claimed to have seen her, too, that night, before her sister disappeared as well.

The sister would have known. The sister saw the ghost, or at least a premonition, perhaps, when we were all following the corpse's tracks.

Death is a message. It has meaning. This is how I've come to understand it, when I think of the killings, and the way that some women and girls are taken. All over the world, not just here in our community, women and girls are taken all the time, sometimes even men and boys are taken. Just taken, they disappear like prey. There has to be a message in it. Meaning. Something we can all learn, some wisdom to impart to the living after we have discovered knowledge from the dead.

◊　◊　◊

When I think of the ghost of the first girl, I think of the cadaver dogs that worked with the searchers and spent so many days trying to find her body. I think of those loyal dogs trained to recover human remains. I even went so far as to speak to the police about the dogs, to see if I could adopt the cadaver dogs when they were no longer fit to work, when it was time for the dogs to retire.

Years after the search, the police were more than happy to give the retired cadaver dogs to me. The dogs had served the public well and were in need of a good home, being old and no longer fit to work such long hours.

I'm glad I have the dogs with me now, mainly because I love them and they are good pets, loyal and intelligent. But also for other reasons, because I've seen the other ghost, the new ghost, the ghost of you, my little sister, and I know you're waiting for someone to find your body.

◊　◊　◊

Retired cadaver dogs make good pets for women who fear being murdered by misogynistic serial killers suffering from the worst type of blood lust. The dogs can find you long after you're gone, a stranger even to yourself, rotting in the oversized luggage, carry-on of carrion, a host like a giant hotel for bacteria. The brutal people who might want to take you away from your life—photograph you, cage you, and use you like an object—are holistic in the killer's design. Without ever touching a hair on your body, they speak the feminist heresy of maltreated husbands and fathers, outraged boyfriends who think in patters of coded brutality, ever so abstract as feces, faces, fences, and stories never read by the instigated, lines written, gored in veil.

◇ ◇ ◇

Veiled in gore, I'm saving these retired cadaver dogs for me and for you and for every woman and girl who might be taken. The dogs' eyes are never as beautiful as they are now, when they are sent away from the field, no longer deemed fit enough for working, retired with no one but me to want them and to love them, no one else but me to suffer them a home. Because who else would? Who would want a pet trained to know how you stink as your corpse decays, a pet trained in all the stages, the ways of finding and knowing, responding to the dead to please the living?

◇ ◇ ◇

Men like your killer have excellent reasons for constructing a den of horror to make you forget who you are. What you are has come to him in the corner of a room where I think I know how men feel when indignation awaits those who show sympathy to the delinquent. That beautiful face like a woman whose eyes are rumors of god!

◇ ◇ ◇

Your killer is a whine-fucker who scowls, screaming hysterically at every woman who was tender to his first victim in the room in the corner, where no one else but women and girls showed sympathy to the delinquent.

◇ ◇ ◇

The delinquent asks, as it were, for a love story for misunderstood women, by remembering her killer tearing her apart. Unholy joy touches someone every twenty minutes, too short a window to take a backseat. If the world was a paperweight under glass, she was sorry she saw it, sorry to have held it in her hand to behold it. Her whole face changed in the reflection in that room where he held her, a tiny teenage runaway ushered through the gates of hell. You still want to be the first one through the door, the hero of this little girl?

◊ ◊ ◊

Let me stay tame for a while, waiting in my makeshift coffin, resting on the floor of the rickety old car, after putting out the fire in the barn near the abandoned cabin where you once lay, a stranger to the night.

◊ ◊ ◊

Under glass, the window snow globe, under mirror, your true-face mask under a veil of tears, the most handsome bride, the way strangers wanted to kiss you as you walked to church and disappeared before your wedding. Later, everyone thought you had run away. As guests waited in the chapel, August sun shone vacant over the land of love like a dissimilar identical twin to your neglected kingdom. Knighted by the moon, showing no restraint, howling, you punish your former self by defacing a photograph where you stand near the cabin's fire escape, near the gangling arms of an eight-year-old girl, perhaps wondering, how long? How long?

◊ ◊ ◊

The man who took you says his name is Charles. Charles whispers, *here I am. Here I am. I am here.* A pathetic thing even before he became a killer, he had to keep clawing upside down to dig a cellar. I see his handsome face transforming again in dreams. The last man in the gale at the gate, hid, a stranger behind his eyes. I asked the coachman coming behind his eyes, my running murmur miserable.

◊ ◊ ◊

On flooded roads, my retired cadaver dogs swim to find you, long after everyone else has given up the search for your body. No one else ever finds you, not even in dreams.

◊ ◊ ◊

On flooded roads, down a hillside, you escape in a mattress floating on brown waters.

DRIFTWOOD SISTERS

Through trees reflected on dark waters, she looked up
but couldn't hear songbirds over the engine's hum. His words
faded as he caught the anchor and secured it inside the boat,
afterwards dabbing his forehead with a small white towel.
Farmland was lost under waves below treetops, children sitting on the roof of a barn, waving to her before bathing
their faces and arms in the boat's wake. Under waves, mock-
ingbirds hid and fluttered. From a distance, water played
tricks on her ears. He spoke to her in strained tones under-
water where the needle etched his name across her thigh, the
needle that once read dust from his hands and banjo music
on the scratched records in his grandfather's collection. He
said it was enough—not to hear but to listen for her sisters'
voices echoing across submerged houses. Moments after the
children dove under a makeshift bridge of tires and drift-
wood, the engine stalled near silver maples beyond the drain

field. "I will speak to you, again," she cried only after they were gone. Her voice was a thin string, the clear strong line that could not be broken by the fisherman. The line wound around and around the stark trees as the moon brightened. The caught hook dangled high above a crane's nest like a hypnotist's gaudy charm. He reached for his banjo, and his pupils constricted with the bright beams of boat light approaching. His trembling broke the music, and he changed the melody as they drifted along. Only she could hear the shore turn and the bones creaking in drowned girls' slender arms that seemed never to still. As she dove away, he winked at her, his eye blue-green flecked with yellow-gray like the hay that had caught in her mother's hair as women in church dresses floated to the far bank, their hands like little oak limbs pointing toward evening.

THE LISTENER

Behind the broken rails of the white fence, she moved, startling the deer. Near the cattails, she fed scraps to the dogs tied to the east wall near her sister's face at the window, sweet breath fogging smudged glass. Every spring, the pond encroached upon the house after the rains, deer drinking from its murky edge where paint flecks floated, breaking apart on bark, leaves, and bottles filled with air. Styrofoam clashed with embers in the wind's wake, the cup torn apart. The dogs swam under their leashes to chase bits of biscuit floating out the door to the water. Mayflies skimmed the surface and clung to the window screens. As she watched the wings' shadow cross her sister's face, she didn't have anything to say. Even when she left the house, she would not speak to her brother in words. From her sister to her mother to her father's sun-darkened hands, vases, coffee cups, sugar cubes, and teaspoons were dried and exchanged in silence. Watching the dogs at the window, she often became confused and used her mouth for the wrong reasons. Her teeth were like her hands, another way to grasp and carry necessary items from the rooms to the windows and back. Venturing out into the half-immersed porch to sit on the swing in sunlight, she let her feet move in and out of the pond water. Crouching low as she swung, she amused her sister inside, feeding the dogs bread from her mouth. They leapt up to her lips delicately as in a kiss. Their paws splashed back into the water as they carried the bread away, quickly so that the others wouldn't steal the crumbs. Fingers were a last resort. Her sister didn't trust them to touch faces as she trusted a mouth no longer used for speaking. Stumbling toward the window, she pressed her face against the screen to feel the mayflies lighting on her cheek. Sometimes her hands like the deer could be forgotten, even by the ones who waited for their return.

WHITE CLOTH

I was raised by a ghost whose voice was the moon, a ghost whose mouth moved without sound to make rain—the lover and the dreamer, the stillborn daughter. Hands on my face, shoes dripping oil, why was the ghost dancing? Near a dusty mirror, Mommy cried for Daddy, that cowboy who lived in another woman's garage.

What did the ghost want? A ruined gown dragging through dirt, used, twirling in the dark, a woman in white behind the arched doorway, firelight on burnt catfish, the color of singed lace near flame?

Beetles ran to the fountain trickling green water. Silence was a birdcage the ghost strummed, that makeshift violin in the evenings, slants as delicate as bone—frames of girlhood hunger.

Twenty years away from this night, I twirl. A beggar with scarred eyelids throws ancient coins at my feet. Palms open on air. Blue flies land on broken fingers. The dead woman's thighs reveal a thin and filthy line, ants crawling over spilled syrup.

Now reflections light on white cloth over a tall bottle of golden liquor. Shadows lace my fingers, the dim-lit bar. The ghost releases me. The fading cowboy waits in a lonely room, paralyzed by the memory of the bull.

"Here are my lips. Here is my hand. Take it," he whispers. And I whisper old dreams as light as the tobacco stains on his withered fingers, water on my face, girls in lace dresses, hairless hands as soft as a doe's belly, as soft as fresh bread.

Love isn't a word the ghost remembers, my face in the hospital window, my mommy's face, changing into light. The word for us is gone—a mad dog running through dark streets. A fly swimming in neglected coffee jumps the mirror, cold glass as useless as imagination.

My hands snag the black lines in the back of the dead woman's stockings. In dreams, my daddy could have tortured any of his women until she said his name, until she took his shirt off and examined the stitched chest, her hands wandering.

What scarred secrets one might find! In this light where the ghost's stares are cruel, the respirator makes strange mechanical music. I love the music the way I love Mommy's lost dream. Treacherous in her grief, she once ran away and swam the ocean to a bright stage, a ring of orange globes burning at her feet, glossy floor, still puddle of frozen rain mirroring her legs.

Outside the bar, the highway ran through the old park. In night windows, skin glittered with sweat that would freeze on the harlot's arms, her pale forehead a crust of ice diamonds. There are other places that nameless women go to die, to be forgotten—the riverbank gates rusted shut, blue light wavering across water.

Do all ghosts waver like light? I don't, and yet I want illumination, the voice of skillful surgeons in darkness, the hospital elevator's drowsy sound of sea, lamps in waiting rooms as pale as searchlights combing waters. Now, how do I recognize the cowboy's body? Take smoke and mirrors, a dancer's disguise. Like every performer I ever knew, the first time my daddy walked out of the rodeo arena, he came running back, torn bills turning to powder in his palms.

Shame is passion used to mock sorrow, bloodstains on the carpet, holes in the dressing room walls. A hand like Mommy's touches many people. A hand like Daddy's changes with time.

I can do whatever I want except for make this body move.

I rub my face against his hands, attempting to unlock the old door.

The ghost is dancing.

I steal the key to the abandoned house. But the key won't open the golden room lit with rose globes burning, fingers running along a cherrywood table, taking time to examine even air.

THE LOST SEA

So much of the sea is now farmland. Fishermen no longer fish with cyanide but stare down at tannin-stained waters. Hungry children become displaced on cracked earth while in distant oceans, fish still live in neon cities, the leafy sea dragons and schools of silver hatchet fish swirling elegant sharks. I know nothing of the sharks or the deep blue. I toss the last of our sea monkeys down the low-flush toilet because they are living and dying too fast in graying water for me to understand what the hell sea monkeys are. Guppies? Tadpoles? Listening for the flush, I drop the jar into the trash and then stare into my eyes in the mirror, remembering. You don't seem to like what you remember, my eyes. I'm drowning in sorrow on our old waterbed as you drown in time like water. Every lake is a miniature ocean, you told me once. I once washed my hair in an ancient sea where baby green turtles still swim. Sea ice melts in my rose wine, a thousand yards from the receding shore. Sweating the river, the shallow swells, pulling the ocean inside us to the landscape's evolution, huge boulders once climbed by my ancestors, jumpers of volcanic cliffs falling into the deep beneath the tides, slipping through the swarms, feeding rainwaters for a desert world.

SCRUTINIZE

When the population of earth reached thirty-five billion, a multi-national corporation and jewelry maker called Scrutinize developed a patented proprietary process for converting eyes into jewels. Because the wealthiest one-percent weren't satisfied with owning jewels created from bionic eyes, collectors wanted something rare. Jewels made from real human eyes—especially the eyes of children—were considered the most valuable and highly sought-after.

In those days, when the most beautiful jewelry was made of children's eyes, every major city had a House of the Blind. In this house lived eyeless people who had sold their eyes in their childhood, usually in order to provide a better life for their families. The eyeless usually lived in the House of the Blind for three to ten years, this being the typical time it took to grow, harvest, and transplant customized bionic eyes. Sadly, some donors refused bionic eyes and spent the rest of their lives dreaming of the eyes they had lost.

One particular collector named Miss Goff owned more children's eyes than anyone in the world. In her collection of more than 20,000 eyes, she had rings, earrings, necklaces, bracelets, brooches, anklets, and hair jewelry. She never left her house wearing fewer than a hundred eyes. She collected eyes of all colors—every shade of blue, green, brown, teal, hazel, and violet. She coordinated her eyes to match her outfits. She prided herself on having only the best eyes, but she was discouraged by owning so many duplicate colors. Whenever she met a family with children, she stared into the little ones' faces to see if they might offer something new to her collection. Were the eyes beautiful? Were they kind? Would they be pleasant to gaze into on an ordinary day? Would they look fetching with her wardrobe? Would they provide something unusual, something new?

Families brought their children to her, hoping she would want their eyes. Because she was a true collector, she offered the best prices. In fact, her collection was of international renown, and it was seen as a great honor for a family to have the eyes of its children among her jewels.

However, Miss Goff began to find it tedious to deal with children who were already born. There just wasn't enough variety. She felt as if she had seen all the eyes before. Nothing seemed exceptional, and yet she still had money to spend and wanted to enhance her collection, to allow it to truly grow and evolve. Thinking of the collection as a living thing that was almost like a child, she felt the collection owned her, instead of the other way around.

Assisting Miss Goff, a Scrutinize sales rep download-
ed coded photographs that would allow Miss Goff to create customized eyes, the hypothetical result of couplings
by strangers in the photographs she viewed. She could run
the program two ways—first by creating digitalized results
of couplings or, second, by viewing projected images of future eyes that were possible combinations of human pairings
created by potential donors whose genetic information was
coded into the photographs. If she saw a pair of eyes she
wanted, Scrutinize would contact the male donor and the female donor needed for that specific pairing.

Strangers to each other, each donor in a matched pair
had two choices: (1) to provide genetic material that would be
used to grow a child in a surrogate mother or (2) to procreate
by natural means so that the woman who carried the child
would give it up for adoption at birth. The second option was
the one that earned the highest pay, especially for the woman,
as Miss Goff wanted to follow her jewelry from the moment
of conception and to keep the process as natural as possible.
The child would be raised in the House of the Blind until
its fifth birthday, when its eyes would be harvested for Miss
Goff's collection.

For her fortieth birthday, which was six years away, Miss
Goff wanted a pair of eyes so beautiful and so unusually
bright they would be unlike any other. This pair of eyes had
been discovered after numerous digital pairings of random
males and females of all ages, nationalities, races, religions,
and creeds. The pair resulted from the coupling of a blue-
eyed Navajo girl and a green-eyed Persian man in his late
forties. The product of their union had a 96.55556783434

percent chance of producing a child with the most amazing sky-blue eyes full of flecks of gold.

When Miss Goff found the digital rendering of that pair of eyes, she contacted her buyer and representative at Scrutinize. This started an intricate process. The company began contacting the donors and arranging medical tests along with prolonged legal negotiations, delicate and precise in nature. The complications were numerous. The Persian was married with four children, and his wife did not want him to undergo the process of natural conception. However, a price was finally agreed upon.

The girl was a more difficult matter. Only fourteen, she had lied about her age on her application, but parental consent was granted as long as the family got top dollar for natural conception. The girl's mother and father would be present in the conception room, as would the male donor's wife, the nurse, the doctor, the sales rep, and Miss Goff, who would have the best seat, nearest the bed.

When it came to ensuring the color of the eyes, many factors had to be controlled—the precise day and time, the correct dosage of hormones and vitamins administered over the course of several months, the temperature of the conception room, and the achievement of both male and female orgasm to ensure a most viable pregnancy. Yet, even with all these factors carefully regulated, there were no guarantees. Sometimes the color of the eyes didn't come out as predicted and the process had to start all over again.

Miss Goff was a meticulous, scrupulous collector. She would not be satisfied with anything other than the particular eyes she had requested. To be certain that everything was being done to her standards, Miss Goff wanted to be part of the entire process. "I'm paying," she said to the doctor and the girl. "This is my baby, too. I deserve to experience its every stage. This is, after all, part of what I'm paying for."

"Yes, yes," the Scrutinize sales associate said. He was an eager little man, thin, balding with bushy eyebrows, and narrow birdlike eyes. Miss Goff wanted to blame him for his eagerness, a quality she never liked in men, but she reminded herself that when half of the world's population was starving, starvation tended to create a certain eagerness in people. She counted on that eagerness in the pursuit of her passions.

"I'd like some more time with the girl," said Miss Goff.

The girl looked at Miss Goff with her Navajo blue eyes, and Miss Goff wondered if they were for sale.

"She'll be available shortly after her exam," said the doctor.

Miss Goff booked a table at a tearoom near the hospital so that she and the girl could have tea after the examination was over. During the gynecological procedure, the girl tried not to look at Miss Goff, who was staring at her eyes and talking about tea. The doctor informed Miss Goff that everything was normal, the girl healthy, fertile, and her eggs viable.

Later at the tearoom, Miss Goff was smiling at the Navajo girl. "What lovely eyes you have."

"Thank you," the girl said, refusing the cup of oolong offered to her.

"I don't suppose your eyes are for sale?"

"No."

"You're a virgin?"

"I told the doctor."

"You understand what's expected?"

"They explained it."

"You're willing to suffer the pains of birth and to relin-
quish the child to the House of the Blind?"

"I am."

"Why?"

"You're paying enough money to feed, clothe, and shelter my family for the rest of our lives. Enough left over so
that I can have a child of my own. One day."

"It is a wonderful opportunity, isn't it?"

"Yes."

"You realize how lucky you are?"

"I do."

"I offered you the best price for everything."

"I know."

"But you haven't thanked me?"

"I'm sorry."

"Well?"

"Thank you, Miss Goff."

Miss Goff smirked and finished her tea. She wouldn't
see the girl again for several months.

The next time they saw each other would be in the
conception room, where the girl tried not to look at anyone, especially not at the nude Persian, who seemed old,
jittery, and nervous—so very nervous that Miss Goff began to wonder if he would be capable of inseminating the
girl.

Inside the conception room, the girl undressed, staring
at the white walls. She did as she was told, obeying the doctor's orders without question. Nude and splayed on the bed

before the man, she waited in silence for him to penetrate her. In the presence of all witnesses, including the doctor, the nurse, her mother and father, the man's wife, the sales rep, and Miss Goff, she arranged herself.

"All right," the doctor said, checking the thermostat and removing a stopwatch from his lab coat pocket. "Watch the time. Let's get this show on the road."

The conception began precisely as scheduled, yet Miss Goff was disappointed by the apparent lack of female orgasm. In fact, she would later blame this lack of female orgasm for what went wrong the first time when the pregnancy didn't take.

During the second attempt, the doctor seemed bored by the entire procedure. "With all the over population, it's a shame to bring another child into the world," he said, when the girl attempted to push the man away.

"Nurse, help her," the doctor said as the girl struggled against the man.

The nurse gave the girl a shot and then repositioned her on the bed, her legs spreading wider as the nurse placed her feet into stirrups. The girl's knees fell back.

"Okay, get on with it. We're falling behind schedule," said the doctor to the man. Then, the doctor said to the sales rep, "At least the child will be well provided for, will never hunger. For a while, it will be blind, that's all."

"But Miss Goff has promised to pay for the best bionic eyes," the sales rep said to the doctor while using his most cheery voice.

"True," said the doctor. "The transplant should allow the child to see again, in several years' time, after the harvest."

"You promise?" the Persian asked, now finished with his duty and removing himself from the semi-conscious girl. "You promise the child will have bionic eyes?"

"Don't trouble Miss Goff," the sales rep said to the nude man, who sluggishly gathered his clothes, every now and then turning to regard the girl with a look of regret-tinged horror. "Miss Goff has been very generous. Everything is clearly stated in the contract. Read it."

The Persian dressed and began to leave the room with his wife. "Is that all?" he asked the doctor, giving one last concerned glance to the girl, still tied down on the bed.

"Yes, for you," the doctor said. "You've done your part. Now, go."

"Will I be contacted?" asked the man. His wife, holding his hand, attempted to pull him out of the conception room.

"About what?" asked the doctor.

"The birth of the child."

"Certainly not."

"Read the contract!" the sales rep said. "Any attempt to find or to contact the child will constitute breach of contract. It will start a chain of legal reactions that you will not want to deal with."

At that, the Persian left with his wife.

The nurse checked on the girl on the table. "We just need to keep you here for a little while longer. Try to relax. You did fine. Keep your legs elevated."

The girl began to cry softly. At first, Miss Goff thought she was laughing.

"We're all done here, Miss Goff," the doctor said. "You may go anytime you like."

"Good," said Miss Goff, staring at the weeping girl. "Hopefully, this one will take."

"I'll keep you posted about the follow-up exams and ultrasounds. You may, of course, attend those procedures."

Miss Goff said, "I don't want to miss anything, not even a single blood test."

"As you wish."

Miss Goff kept up with the girl and all her examinations throughout the pregnancy. She even attended the birth of the child, a little girl. Shortly after the birth, Miss Goff studied the child and was disappointed to see that the color of the eyes wasn't quite right. The eyes were an ordinary shade of blue, showing none of the brilliance of the gold flecks in the projection.

"Have patience," the doctor said. "As you know, children's eyes change over time. An infant's eyes aren't always an exact predictor of what color a child's eyes will be."

"You better hope that's the case here," said Miss Goff. "I have no use for eyes the color of this infant's eyes."

By the time the child reached three years of age, Miss Goff visited her in the House of the Blind only to discover that the color of her eyes still wasn't right. Furious, Miss Goff left. She returned a year and a half later, just before the child's fifth birthday when its eyes were due to be harvested.

"Where is she?" Miss Goff asked, not knowing how to recognize the child among the other seeing children in the House of the Blind, as so many were waiting for their eyes to be harvested. "Where's the one I paid for?"

"Her name," the matron said, "is Angel. She is still a seeing child for now."

"Yes," said Miss Goff. "And she might remain a seeing child forever if her eyes don't turn out the way I was promised."

"Oh, no. We can't have that," said the matron. "If her eyes aren't harvested, she cannot remain in the House of the Blind."

"Has she no place else to go?"

"No," the matron said as she shoved a small intelligent-looking girl into the room where Miss Goff waited. Miss Goff leaned down and pulled Angel toward her. She held Angel's face in her hands, stared into her blue eyes, and said, "Maybe someone else will want them. They are of no use to me. Who would want eyes like these? Ordinary eyes?"

Angel said, "I want them."

"You?" Miss Goff asked. "What on earth would you want with such ordinary eyes? Plain blue eyes!"

"I could use them to see."

"Well, there's that," Miss Goff said, embarrassed as the thought had not occurred to her until now.

"Please, Miss Goff. Can I keep my eyes?" Angel asked.

"Absolutely not," the matron said, looking at Miss Goff with her impersonal bionic eyes.

"Your mother has already sold them," said Miss Goff with exceeding patience as she tried to explain to the child what she assumed the child should already know. "They're not your eyes. You can't keep what's not yours. I paid for them. I bought them before you were born."

"Oh," said Angel. "You did?"

"I thought they already explained such things to you children? Don't you know why you've been living in the House of the Blind?"

"I did wonder. Because I can see."

"The eyes in your head, child, are not your eyes," said the matron. "They are Miss Goff's and have always been hers. She's only letting you borrow them for a little while so she can decide what to do with them."

"I'm starting to think I don't want them after all," said Miss Goff.

"But if you don't want them, and I do—" Angel said.

"You would have never existed, if it weren't for my wanting your eyes in the first place. Angel? Did you ever think of that? I'm the reason you were born," Miss Goff said.

"And why were you born, Miss Goff?" Angel asked.

Miss Goff hesitated, uncertain of how or if she should answer. Finally, she said, "I was born because a woman who was almost as wealthy as I am today wanted my face."

"What do you mean?" asked Angel, whose voice rose and squeaked in a way that sounded frustrated or angry.

"Under this mask, I have no face," said Miss Goff.

But the girl was confused because Miss Goff wasn't wearing a mask. She had a face, a woman's face. Slowly, Angel began to realize it was the face of another woman, a facial accessory that Miss Goff wore along with all her jewelry made of children's eyes. Nothing on the woman was natural or her own.

"Somewhere there's another woman wearing my face," Miss Goff said.

"And somewhere soon there will be a woman wearing my eyes," Angel said.

"Or a man."

"Where's the woman wearing your face, Miss Goff? I want to see her."

"So do I," said Miss Goff. "I'm told the face I was born with was lovely, but I can't remember it. I was only allowed to keep it until I was seventeen. That was so many years ago that I can't really recall. Imagine! I can't remember my own face—my real face."

"Don't you have any photos?" asked Angel.

"I wasn't allowed to keep photos. That was part of the contract."

"What about the woman who has your face? Can't you visit her? Can't you buy it back?"

"No, child, no. That's forbidden. I'm not allowed to have any contact with her, nor am I allowed to know her name. But the money she spent on harvesting my face gave me the chance to become who I am today. I bought another face from another woman and this face has served me well."

"As will my bionic eyes," said Angel.

"Exactly, dear child," Miss Goff said. "You are even more intelligent than you seem. I would like to visit you from time to time, if it's all right?"

"I would like that, very much, especially when I'm blind," Angel said.

In the years to come, in the time of Angel's blindness when she was waiting for her bionic eyes, Angel and Miss Goff began to talk to each other, to really talk. They became friends, and Miss Goff eventually removed Angel from the House of the Blind in order to adopt her as her own daughter.

Even though Miss Goff felt guilty whenever she gazed into Angel's empty eye sockets, she felt she had done the right thing. She and Angel were growing to better understand each other as only a mother and daughter could. During their long conversations, when Angel said how much she missed her eyes, Miss Goff could finally admit how much she missed her face and could almost begin to describe something of its essence.

The memory of her lost face made her cry, and Angel attempted to comfort her. "It will be all right, Mother," Angel said. She reminded Miss Goff that this was just the way life was: only the highborn could afford to keep what they were born with, and there was nothing anyone could do about it.

Women's bodies, along with the bodies of children, handsome men, boys, and girls, were bought and sold, piece by piece, and had been ever since the dawn of time.

ACKNOWLEDGMENTS

Grateful acknowledgment is made to the following publications in which some of these stories have appeared:

North American Review

Fiction International

Santa Fe Literary Review

The Laurel Review

Denver Quarterly

The Collagist

Atticus Review

Lake Effect

PP/FF: An Anthology

CPSIA information can be obtained
at www.ICGtesting.com
Printed in the USA
FFOW04n2039180117
31508FF